THE BOY WHO SWITCHED OFF THE SUN

Written by **Paul Brown**

Illustrated by **Mark O'Hanlon**

FOR KAREN AND SAFFRON
MY TWO FAVOURITES! — PB

FOR ISAAC — MO

First published in Great Britain in 2015
by Fourth Wall Publishing
2 Riverview Business Park,
Shore Wood Road, Bromborough,
Wirral, Merseyside CH62 3RQ

Copyright ©Fourth Wall Publishing 2015

ISBN:978-1-91-085102-9

fourth wall
publishing

Little Marcel didn't just like ice cream,
he absolutely, completely LOVED the stuff!

In fact, he loved it so much, he had secret stockpiles
hidden in every corner of his house.

TOYS

Mr Whippy

He liked nothing more than enjoying a big, delicious scoop while sat on his favourite bench by the beach.

But there was a problem.
A very BIG problem — the SUN!

Its hot, sweltering rays always turned
his delicious, frozen treat into a dripping, mushy mess
long before he could finish it!

Marcel tried EVERYTHING!

He tried eating his ice cream so fast that it didn't have time to melt,
but that only made big, sticky splodges fly everywhere.

He ate it in the frosty-cold,
but that just gave him
horrible brr-brr-brain freeze!

And he even tried eating
it in the dark of night,
but that was far too scary!

Then from out of nowhere, he had an amazing idea!

The sun was just like an enormous, dazzling light bulb dangling in the sky.

"That's it!" shouted Marcel. "I'll just switch off the sun!"

But the sun was millions and millions of miles away...

...Marcel would need to build a superfast, solar-powered space rocket if he was ever going to travel that far.

So, after weeks of building, banging, drilling and clanging...

...he proudly added the finishing touch to his gleaming spacecraft.

That night, Marcel was so excited, he hardly slept a wink.

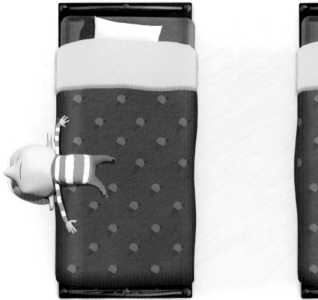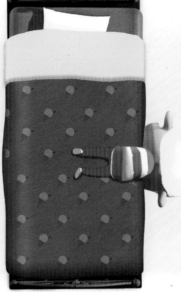

Next morning he leapt out
of bed and ran down to prepare
for launch — it was perfect
rocket-flying weather!

"All systems are ready for lift off"
announced Marcel, as the onboard computer
began its countdown sequence...

5,4,3,2,1...
BLAST OFF!

The powerful rocket blasted higher and higher,
up through the clouds and out into space.

Up amongst the stars, he could see the Earth disappearing into the distance. Marcel thought it looked amazing — just like a great big, fluffy scoop of bubblegum and pistachio ice cream.

By the time they finally reached the sun, planet Earth seemed like a tiny dot in space. Marcel could see the giant 'OFF' switch and quickly set to work.

Floating closer and closer, he could feel the powerful heat washing over him and he wished he had some yummy ice cream to cool him down!

Then he pushed and pushed with all
his strength, until with one huge effort
(and a little help from his dog!)...

KER-LUNK!

...Marcel SWITCHED OFF THE SUN!

But as he set off for home, the sunlight faded fast and his solar-powered rocket began to run out of fuel — spiralling out of control!

Luckily, Marcel managed to crash-land safely back into his garden.

That night, very tired from his long journey, Marcel had lovely dreams about enjoying his favourite treat by the beach — without it melting away!

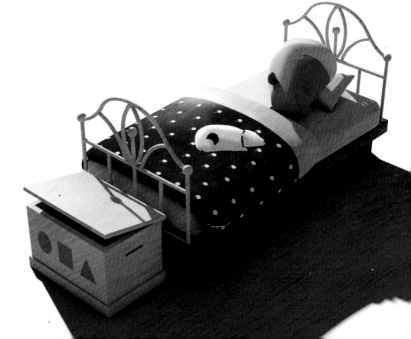

But when Marcel awoke the next morning, all was not well. It was still very dark and scary, and far too cold to eat ice cream.

And much worse than that, terrible things began to happen all around the world...

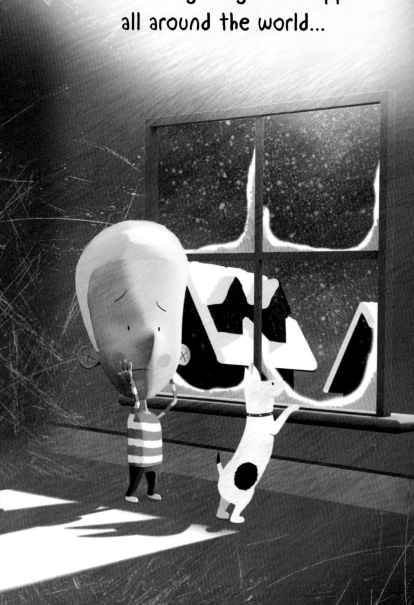

NEWS EXPRESS

FLOWERS AND FORESTS DYING

OH NO!

Marcel realised he'd made
the BIGGEST mistake of all time!

He must switch the sun back on
without delay.

But without the sun's energy,
his solar-powered rocket
just wouldn't work.

He needed to think of a
solution — and quickly!

POWER

And there was one thing that always helped Marcel
to think more clearly — Strawberry Cheesecake ice cream!

As he tucked into a super-sized scoop, the idea suddenly struck him!

He would build a giant catapult to fire an enormous ball of
ice cream straight at the sun's 'ON' switch.

Marcel worked late into the night, building a scoop the size of a house!

It was so utterly enormous, it used up his entire stockpile of ice cream, so he knew he would only have one shot at the sun!

Finally, everything was ready.
Crowds of people came from near and far,
all desperately hoping that Marcel would be
able to switch the sun back on.

"Commence countdown!" he yelled.

5,4,3,2,1...
FIRE!

Everybody watched in wonder as the giant
ball of deliciousness hurtled towards the sun.

"Oh, no!" shouted Marcel.

The ice cream was starting to melt as
it zoomed towards the sun's dying heat...

...And as it got closer, more and more just melted away, until all that remained was a frozen scoop of Tutti Frutti.

Everyone held their breath as the solid,
icy chunk landed a direct hit at the sun's
'ON' switch...

...But nothing seemed to happen!

Had Marcel's plan failed?

Angry and disappointed, the crowd
started to walk away.

Then suddenly, the sky was filled with the brightest light anyone had ever seen!

HURRAY!

Everyone cheered and ran, dancing into the streets!

The next day, all around the world,
everything began to return to normal...

NEWS EXPRESS

FLOWERS & FORESTS
COME ALIVE!

DAILY TIMES

WORLD'S OCEANS DEFROST

EVENING GAZETTE

ANIMALS COME OUT OF HIDING!

And although it was a drippy, melting mess, Marcel was VERY HAPPY to be sitting on his favourite bench enjoying his ice cream...

...and so was his dog.